THE LION
AND THE MOUSE
AF372551

ONCE UPON A TIME, THERE WAS A LION WHO, BESIDES BEING THE KING OF THE JUNGLE, WAS KNOWN FOR BEING VERY BRAVE. ONE DAY, AFTER EATING, HE FELL ASLEEP.

SUDDENLY, A LITTLE MOUSE FOUND HIM ON THE WAY AND, BEING CURIOUS, APPROACHED.

THE LITTLE MOUSE WAS IMPRESSED BY THE LION'S SIZE AND THOUGHT IT WOULD BE FUN TO CLIMB ON HIM. SO, THE SMALL RODENT STARTED RUNNING AND JUMPING ON THE BIG ANIMAL'S BACK.

HOWEVER, WHEN HE LEAST EXPECTED IT,
THE KING OF THE JUNGLE WOKE UP,
LEAVING HIM VERY SCARED.

THE LION, SUSPICIOUS, ASKED WHAT THE MOUSE WAS DOING THERE.

THE SMALL RODENT EXPLAINED THAT HE WAS JUST PLAYING AND ASKED THE FELINE NOT TO HURT HIM.

THE LION BEGAN TO ROAR VERY LOUDLY AND SAID HE WOULD DEVOUR THE MOUSE, SCARING HIM EVEN MORE.

WITHOUT KNOWING WHAT TO DO, THE SMALL RODENT BEGGED THE LION NOT TO EAT HIM AND SAID THAT IF HE WERE SET FREE, HE COULD HELP HIM WHENEVER HE NEEDED.

THE KING OF THE JUNGLE LET GO OF THE MOUSE AND STARTED LAUGHING...

...BECAUSE HE COULDN'T UNDERSTAND HOW SUCH A TINY ANIMAL COULD DO ANYTHING FOR HIM.

AFTER A WHILE, THE MOUSE WAS WALKING THROUGH THE JUNGLE WHEN HE HEARD A VERY LOUD ROAR.

UPON REALIZING IT WAS THE LION, HE BECAME WORRIED AND STARTED LOOKING FOR WHERE THE SOUND WAS COMING FROM.

SUDDENLY, THE MOUSE FOUND THE LION TRAPPED IN A TRAP LEFT BY HUNTERS.

AT THAT MOMENT, HE BEGAN TO GNAW ON THE ROPES WITH GREAT STRENGTH, FREEING HIM.

THE LION THANKED THE MOUSE FOR SAVING HIM
AND APOLOGIZED FOR DOUBTING THAT HE, BEING
SMALL, WOULD BE ABLE TO HELP HIM.

AT THAT MOMENT, THE TWO BECAME BEST FRIENDS AND LIVED HAPPILY EVER AFTER.

THE END.